Mary Anne

Stacey

SEA CITY, NJ
PM
JULY

NEW YORK, NY
PM
JULY

Dawn

CHAIN LETTER

Ann M. Martin

SCHOLASTIC INC.
New York Toronto London Auckland Sydney

Library of Congress Cataloging-in-Publication Data

Martin, Ann M., 1955–
  Chain letter / Ann M. Martin.
    p. cm. — (The Baby-sitters Club)
  Summary: While Kristy is in the hospital recovering from an appendectomy, she receives a chain letter for telling secrets, which throughout the summer circulates around the United States to her fellow club members, who are having better summer vacations than Kristy.

[1. Babysitters — Fiction. 2. Clubs — Fiction. 3. Secrets — Fiction. 4. Letters — Fiction.] I. Title. II. Series: Martin, Ann M., 1955– Baby-sitters Club.
PZ7.M3567585Ch   1993
[Fic] — dc20
                              92-44587
                                    CIP
                                    AC

Art direction and book design by Elizabeth B. Parisi

Interior Illustrations

David Tommasino p. 3; Hollie Rubin pp. 4, 10, 26; Madalina Stefan p. 7; FPG International Corp. pp. 11, 17, 23; Nancy Didion p. 13; Jane Chambles-Wright p. 16; Pete Whitehead p. 19; George Ledas p. 22; Michael Garland p. 28; Peggy Tegel p. 30; Barbara Banthien p. 32.

Photo strip illustrations by Angelo Tillery. Cover portraits by Hodges Soileau.

All rubber stamp designs by Robert Bloomberg. © All Night Media, Inc. Used with permission.

Postage stamps copyright © by the United States Postal Service. Used by permission.

Copyright © 1993 by Ann M. Martin.

ISBN 0-590-47151-1

12 11 10 9 8 7 6 5 4 3 2 1   3 4 5 6 7 8/9

Printed in Singapore

First Scholastic printing, September 1993

A note from
Robin

Dear Kristy,

Your mom called to tell us you're in the hospital. Appendicitis — YIKES! At least the operation is over. (We got all the news.)

I bet you're bored so I thought I'd send something to amuse you. My friend Margie sent me this different kind of chain letter. It's about secrets. This is what you have to do:

Divulge a secret to one person. It should be a secret you've never told to a <u>soul</u>. Then that person has to send a secret to one other person, and so on.

If you break the chain — if you don't divulge a secret within 48 hours — you'll have horribly bad luck. This is no joke. Margie knows someone who broke a chain once, and the very next day she failed a Spanish test and fractured her thumb. (You're supposed to have good luck if you don't break the chain.)

Here is my secret: When I was eight, I cracked one of my mom's expensive perfume bottles, and then I told her the dog knocked it over. She still thinks that's what happened.

Okay, your turn!

Get well soon.

Love Robin

Kristy
Room 237
Stoneybrook General Hospital
Rosedale Road
Stoneybrook, CT 06800

Ms. Stacey McGill
321 E. 65th Street
Apt 2F
New York, NY 10000

NEW YORK, N.Y.
AM
JULY

USA
19

Ms. Janine Kishi

MJK

58 Bradfourd Cort
Stoneybrook CT 06800

Hi, sis!

How are you and who are mom and Dad?
I'm fine we're having so much fun in New
York. Today Stace and I whent to the
musem of modorn art. Janine is the BSC
ansering machin working. Could you plese
make sure it is pluged in and the gren
light is on becuase pople might call and
forget about our ~~vac~~ ~~vaca~~ trips. That
is all.

Love, Claudia

P.S. At the musum we saw this old
statu that was missing one arm and
a hunk of its nose why would
someone put somthing lick that in a
musum.

Ms. Mallory Pike
12 Sandpiper Lane
Sea City, New Jersey 08200

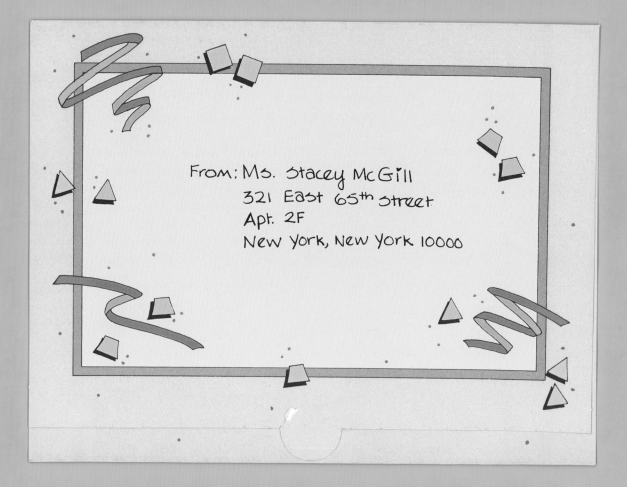

From: Ms. Stacey McGill
321 East 65th Street
Apt. 2F
New York, New York 10000

The famous Hollywood sign, perched high above glamorous, star-studded Los Angeles.

Dear Claud,
  Having a wonderful time.
Wish you were here. Honest!
I asked Mary Anne what
she wants to do while she's
here, and she said, "Go to
Disneyland." I practically
grew up there but we went
anyway, for her sake. We
spent the entire day in
Fantasyland. Jeff said if
he had to ride those teacups
again he'd barf. Peace, Dawn

P.S. Speaking of the teacups-
  I wonder, if you kissed a boy while you were
riding around in them, would your braces lock to-
                                                        gether?

Ms. Claudia Kishi
C/o Mr. Edward
        McGill
321 E. 65th St.
Apt. 2F
New York, NY 10000

Dear Mal,

I knew you copied from me. I saw you peeking over. At first I was mad 😠, but don't worry. We are forever friends. 🙂

Best Friends Forever

Love Jessi

P.S. You probably shouldn't copy anymore.

Ms. Jessi Ramsey
c/o Pike
12 Sandpiper Lane
Sea City, NJ 08200

Giant Panda

USA
29

SEA CITY NJ
AM
JULY

Ms. Mary Anne Spier
c/o Schafer
22 Buena Vista
Palo City, CA 92800

Dear Mr. Postman
or Mrs. Postman,

Deliver
letter
sooner
better
later
letter
madder
I getter!

A beautiful sunset over the Manhattan skyline.

Dear Kristy,

I got your letter, and your secret is safe. I really don't think it's so awful, though. My mom says there are no bad thoughts, only bad actions. Your _thoughts_ aren't going to hurt anybody. Plus, as one divorced kid to another, I can tell you that _I_ don't always think too kindly about _my_ parents. I am still mad at them for splitting up, and sometimes I hate living two different lives in two different cities. (Other times I love it ↓)

I wish you felt better. I don't like to think of you lying around in that hospital worrying.

Claudia says hi and she sends you a hug.

Longer letter later,

Stace

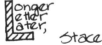

Kristy Thomas
Room 237
Stoneybrook General
            Hospital

Rosedale Road
Stoneybrook, CT 06800

WHILE YOU WERE OUT

TO _the members of the BSC_ TIME _5:45 p.m._

DATE _Monday_

NAME _Mrs. Rodowsky_

COMPANY _____ EXT. _____

PHONE _____

- [x] Telephoned
- [ ] Called to see you
- [ ] Returned your call
- [ ] Please call back
- [ ] Will call again
- [ ] Important

MESSAGE _Mrs. Rodowsky called. Forgot the BSC was closed for vacation. Wanted a sitter Saturday for the boys. Can't wait for you to come home. Hopes you had fun on your various trips. Hopes Kristy is feeling better. (I think your answering machine is on the blink, sweetie. Mrs. Rodowsky called on my line.)_

Mom (Mrs. Kishi)

Mary Anne Spier
C/O Schafer
22 Buena Vista
Palo City, California 92800

Ms. Claudia Kishi
C/O McGill
321 East 65th Street
Apt. #2F
New York, New York 10000

Greetings from Sea City

Dear Stacey,
   Guess who I ~~was~~ saw on the beech today. Toby. He was with a grit girl. She was ugly. A new lifgard is at the beech. He is ugly to. Mal says this is not a nice postcard and I do not have any more rooms so goodby.

   That means I love you, not I love sheep.
      Love,
        Margo Pike

Postcard
Address

Stacey McGill
321 East 65th St.
Apt. 2-F
New York, NY 10000
USA
Planet Earth

SEA CITY, NJ
AM
JULY

19 USA

Ck
% Mcgill
321 E 65th Strt.
Apt. 2F
New York NY 10000

Dawn
22 Buena Vista
Palo City, CA 92800

Ms. Shannon Kilbourne
Camp Eerie
Princeton, MI 48800

My dearest Cam,
I hope I may call
you Cam, even though
I have never met
you. You do not know
me (of course), but I
am your number one fan.
As I write these words to you,
I am on a plane, flying from
California to Connecticut. I am
reminded that not long ago,
when my stepsister and I
were on our way to California,
you were on the plane! But you
were sitting in first class,
and we were way in
the back of the plane. I
wish I could have visited
with you and gotten your
autograph, but I didn't
think I should ask the
flight attendant to open
that curtain.
Anyway, I have been
a fan of yours for years.
I even
Uh-oh, here come our
dinners. I have to put
this away to make
room for my tray.
In case I don't
have a chance to
finish it, I better
sign it now.
I love you!
Your biggest fan,
Mary Anne Spier
XXX OOO

Mallory

i

Claudia

Jessi

NEW YORK, NY
AM
JULY

STAMFORD, CT
AM
AUGUST

Kristy

SEA CITY, NJ
PM
JULY